# Oh, Look!

*Patricia Lee Gauch, editor*

Manufactured in China by South China Printing Co. Ltd. Designed by Semadar Megged. Text set in 20-point Goudy. The illustrations are rendered in pencil and watercolor.

Library of Congress Cataloging-in-Publication Data
Polacco, Patricia. Oh, look! / Patricia Polacco. p. cm. Summary: Three goats visit a fair but run home after they seem to encounter a troll. [1. Goats—Fiction. 2. Fairs—Fiction.] I. Title. PZ7.P75186Oh 2004 [E]—dc22 2003012098
ISBN 0-399-24223-6
10 9 8 7 6 5 4 3 2 1
First Impression

# Oh, Look!

# PATRICIA POLACCO

Philomel Books • New York

Oh, look, we see a fence. It's always there, keeping us in . . . safe and sound.

Can't go over it,
can't go under it,
can't go around it . . .

But there's the gate and it's unlocked.
Let's go through it!
Squeak, squeak, squeak it goes as we go through it.

Oh, look, we see a bridge. A nice wide bridge.
    Can't jump over it,
    can't go under it,
    can't go around it . . .
Let's go across it!
Click, click, click our little hooves go as we go across it.

Oh, look, we see a hill. High and green.
      Can't go over it,
      can't go under it,
      can't go around it . . .
Let's climb up it!
Puff, puff, puff we go as we climb up it.

Oh, look, we see water. A deep blue pond.
    Can't go over it,
    can't go under it,
    can't go around it . . .
Let's swim in it!
Swish, swish, swish we go as we swim in it.

Oh, look, we see some mud. Soft and gooey, slippery and slick.

Can't go over it,
can't go under it,
can't go around it . . .

Let's play with it!

Squish, squish, squish it goes as we play with it.

Oh, look, we see a fair. With big striped tents and flags
all aflutter.

     Can't go over them,
     can't go under them,
     can't go around them . . .
Let's run between them!
Flap, flap, flap go the flags as we run between them.

Oh, look, we see a carousel with merry, merry music,
going round and round.
Can't go over it,
can't go under it,
can't go around it . . .
Let's get on it!
Um-pah-pah, um-pah-pah, um-pah-pah it goes as we
climb on.

Oh, look, we see a mirror. It wiggles and wobbles.
    Can't go over it,
    can't go under it,
    can't go around it . . .
How does it do that? Let's look behind it!

**Oh, look!** We see something . . .
with great big eyes and sharp green claws.
It's an ogre, and he looks mean.
Now we're scared!
Let's run home as fast as we can!

Past the mirror that wiggles and wobbles,
on the carousel that um-pah-pahs!

Between the tents that flap, flap, flap!

Into the water with a swish, swish, swish,
and gooey mud with a squish, squish, squish!

Up the hill with a puff, puff, puff,
across the bridge with a click, click, click!

Through the gate with a long, loud squeak . . .

right back home, safe and sound!
Ahhhhhhhhhh.